The Gift and Other Stories

by

Richard Bryant

Published by Past Historic
6 Church Street, Kings Stanley, Stonehouse,
Gloucestershire, England

ISBN 978 0 9557093 1 9

A catalogue record for this publication is available from the British Library.

Set in 11/13 Palatino with Nueva Std headings
by Past Historic, Stonehouse, Gloucestershire

Cover design by Richard Bryant

The cover image is a detail from a painting by Richard Bryant

Printed and bound in Great Britain by Henry Ling Limited

Contents

The Gift

The Gift

It was a dark, wet night. The Christmas lights in the streets had been up so long that they had ceased to really notice them. The shop windows displayed 'Sale' stickers already, and the shops were so hot that the shoppers wilted every time they entered one.

They were tired, and the only thing that kept them going was the knowledge that they had finally got all they thought they needed.

Afterwards, they couldn't remember what drew their attention to the man standing in the middle of the pedestrianised street. He had a tray, not even a stall like the rest of the street traders. And he wasn't selling; he was trying to give something away. Time and again he would offer whatever it was to shoppers as they brushed past him, but most of them turned away and hurried on. Occasionally, however, someone would stop and accept what the man was holding out.

The two tired shoppers began to give him a wide berth, but there was something about the man that drew them closer. It was difficult to define, like warmth in the cold of the night.

He stepped forward a little.

'Please take one,' he said. 'It is a gift from God'.

'Uh Oh,' they thought. 'A religious nutter'.

They started to shake their heads and smile. But they forgot the cardinal rule which lies behind the smile of rejection – do not look at the other person's face, and especially do not look them in the eye. They looked at the man's strong, quiet face, and their polite rejections died on their lips. Instead they accepted the gift. The man smiled a quite wonderful smile, and tipped his head on one side a little in acknowledgement. Then he turned to offer a gift to another pair of shoppers, but they ostentatiously looked the other way. 'Peace be with you,' the man said, before offering the gift to the next passer-by.

The two shoppers stood still for a moment, in the middle of all the rush, and looked at one another and at the gift that they had received. It was quite small and square, and wrapped in Christmas paper. Eventually they put the gift into one of their bags and walked back to their car. They were quiet as they drove home.

Once at home, however, the bustle of Christmas overtook them again. They unloaded the bags and put the gift under the Christmas tree. Then they threw themselves into the last minute preparations, wrapping presents; preparing the turkey; mending the fairy lights – the usual things.

Eventually, on Christmas Eve, they sank exhausted into their chairs and turned on the telly. They laughed at the comedy. They cried at the sad film. They half listened to the News. And finally, deciding that Terminator 27 was not what they wanted on Christmas Eve, they went to bed.

They must have slept, but it didn't seem like it when the children came in saying:

'Dad, we keep hearing a funny noise!'

Dad was not amused, and, with a few well-chosen and decidedly unfestive words, he got up to send the children back to bed. However, as he came out onto the landing, he too heard a noise from downstairs. It sounded like singing. He went down, pushed open the sitting room door, and stopped in his tracks.

The room was bathed in light, and singing filled the air.

He called to his wife, and soon the whole family was standing just inside the door, listening and looking at the Christmas tree under which the light shone.

Slowly they moved forward. The centre of the light was the stranger's gift. They pulled it out and, rather gingerly, removed the wrapping.

The only words on the actual box were 'Handle With Care'.

They opened the box and found inside a beautiful model of the earth. It was jewel-like in its detail. Across the surface it seemed that real clouds scudded and, as a base note to the sound of singing, they could hear the roar of the sea. The heat of the sun warmed their faces, and the wind laughed through the branches of a billion trees.

The more they looked, the more they saw and

the more they marvelled. If they stared long enough at a particular spot on the globe, the scene became larger so that they could make out more and more details. They could see mountains and rivers, great plains and tiny islands. In, and in, and in they could go – like pressing the magnification button on a microscope.

They could see cities and towns; aeroplanes and ships. They could see elephants and wild horses. They could see penguins and otters. They could see butterflies and flowers. And they could see people. People everywhere.

Gradually the noise of the people made it difficult to hear anything else, so it was some time before they realised that the singing had stopped. But they could not avoid seeing the changes to the globe in their hands. Imperceptibly at first, but with growing pace, the surface of the globe grew dark. Different noises became all too apparent. The thunder of gunfire and explosions; the screams of people and animals; the smell of burning houses; the moans of the starving. There were few trees to stop the wind as it scoured the soil from the bare land and threw it into the dying sea. And overlying all this destruction came the voice of the people, chanting 'Mine. Mine. Mine.'

On and on.

'Mine. Mine. Mine.'

The family were deeply shocked by the changes, and began looking for ways to turn the thing off. They couldn't find any switches, but on the top of the globe there was something like a pyramid. They pushed it, then pulled it up and it came out. It was like a long, heavy iron nail. It seemed so crude in comparison to the intricacy of the globe, but, as it was withdrawn, the globe opened up into four segments that folded down to reveal an exquisite Nativity scene. There were all the usual figures – the ox and ass; the shepherds and wise men; Mary, Joseph and the Baby Jesus in his bed of straw.

And, once again, there was the sound of singing all around them. They were spellbound. The amount of detail on each delicate figure was out of this world. They pushed aside in their minds the blackness that they had watched overwhelm the earth and chose, instead, to focus on the Nativity because they found the beautiful simplicity of the stable easier to cope with.

Throughout the Christmas holidays the Nativity sat on the mantelpiece, and everyone who came admired it. Gradually the family began to think that the strange music in the air, the light in the night, and the disturbing scenes on the globe, had all been a sort of collective dream.

Then, one day, the four segments of the globe slowly began to close up. As they watched, the segments clicked together and the globe was whole again. None of them would swear to it later, but, as the segments came together, it was as if two hands cupped around the globe, carefully, protectively.

They looked for the box to pack the globe away, and only then found the slip of paper that was tucked into the lid. On it was written:

'We hope that you gained pleasure from the Globe, and that it proved provoking. The surface of the Globe has been specially treated. It was protected in the sealed packaging, so that you might enjoy a vision of its unique beauty. However, what you now see is bio-mechanically linked to the state of the real earth.

'It is recommended that each owner allows their Globe to complete its pre-programmed cycle which ends at Easter. The last part of this cycle is triggered on Good Friday when the surface of the Globe will be further darkened by the shadow of the Cross. On that day the Locking Nail should be driven back into the heart of the Globe. We guarantee that what happens next will be truly unique.

'The makers suggest that your Globe, given and received as a gift, should be placed somewhere obvious where you can see it everyday. If you are willing, this Globe has the power to influence your actions from this day on. Our greatest wish is that, one day, you will again see the Globe in all its original splendour. Thank You.'

The family looked at one another, threw the box away, and put the globe back on the mantelpiece with the Locking Nail beside it.

And life was never quite the same again.

The Light in the Desert

The Light in the Desert

Brother George was cold. He was also hungry, thirsty and tired. He had travelled for days through an arid landscape parched brittle by the sun. The ground was dry. The earth crumbled into dust under his feet. Nothing but the toughest plants grew in this landscape, plants with thin leaves and sharp thorns.

Brother George was going to collect books and an icon for the library of his own Friary from the desert monastery of St. Peter. Before he started on this, the last stage of his long journey, he had been told that there were two small villages half way across the desert where he could find refreshment and rest.

The villages stood no more than seven or eight miles apart at either end of a fertile valley where an underground river broke out of its prison of rock to provide life-giving sustenance and good farmland for the two settlements.

You couldn't miss these villages, he was told, because all the roads across the desert led down into the valley. Even in the dark they were visible, because, being Christian communities, they believed that they should keep a light burning at all times, and this acted as a beacon for travellers in the night.

In the desert the transition from day into night is sharp and abrupt. There is little dusk. But Brother George kept going, confident that he was no more than a few miles from the nearest village and that soon he would see their light. As night deepened he walked more slowly, and his pack began to feel heavier and heavier. Still he saw no light. He was puzzled. He felt that perhaps he had taken a wrong turning, even though most of the route had been well marked.

He looked to right and left. Nothing. He trudged on. He must have made a mistake.

Beside the track there was small hill and, in one last attempt to see the light, he climbed slowly to the top.

At first he could see nothing but blackness, but, after a while, he saw the faintest glimmer far away. A light! Reassured and encouraged, he ran down the hill and stepped out with renewed vigour towards the light. Even so it took more than two hours for him to reach the first buildings of the village. He knocked on a door and asked where he might find the guest house.

'Since it is so late,' replied the owner, 'I will take you there myself.' He pulled on some shoes and led Brother George to a building in the middle of the village. It was on top of this building that the beacon light was burning.

The Guest Master welcomed him, showed him to a room and brought him water so that Brother George could wash the grime of the road from his face, and from his hands and feet. Then his host bustled away and returned with food and wine. Brother George ate and drank gratefully, and then he collapsed onto his bed and was quickly asleep.

The following morning he told the Guest Master about his concerns of the night before – the feeling that he had somehow lost his way – and all because he seemed to have miscalculated the distance to the first village.

The Guest master shook his head a little.

'No, my friend, you did not miscalculate. Coming from the direction in which you were travelling, we are the *second* village, I am afraid that you passed right by our neighbours.'

'Then why couldn't I see their light?'

'Probably because it wasn't lit.'

'But I thought that you were both Christian villages,' Brother George said, in some confusion.

'So we are. But lately our neighbours have declared that the shining light should only be seen as part of a special ceremony. They say that it is too precious for every day. So they have decided that their light will only shine for an hour each week, and that time will be on Sunday in the middle of the morning.'

'But,' said Brother George, 'that doesn't make any sense. Surely no one will need or see the light then?'

'Oh people still need it. But you are right, my friend, they cannot see it. And that is not just because the light is less easy to see in the daylight. It is even stranger than you might think, for, when the light is lit, it is not lit on top of the guest house any more, but inside so that only those gathered there can see it. It doesn't seem quite right to me. But there, I expect they have their reasons. And they are good people, mind you. If you were travelling during the day, or you happened to find them by chance at night, they would still offer you hospitality. Generous to a fault they are. Its just this business about their light that leaves us a bit puzzled.'

By nine o'clock in the morning Brother George was ready to start the second half of his desert journey, and he was waved away with smiles, and a full pack and water bottle. Two villagers even went some of the way with him, worried that he was travelling alone.

The road climbed up out of the valley, and, at the top, he turned round for one last look. In the distance he could just see the village that he had missed in the night. He admired the generosity of spirit of his host, but he couldn't help but feel that the villagers who hid their light away were missing the point badly.

After a while he turned from the valley and sighed. The two villagers who had offered to accompany him nodded and smiled, as puzzled as he was. Then they stepped out together on their journey.

Visions

Visions

She was very old. But Wisdom had long been a friend, and the youngsters came to listen, and to ask her about things.

'Tell us about visions,' they said, in that mixture of request and challenge that is such a crucial part of being young.

'Ah,' she said, 'visions is it? Well, visions are powerful things. And they are strange, unlike anything else – at the same time vividly real and yet beyond our normal reality.

Visions are not something that only happened in the past, nor, whatever some may say, are they simply figments of particular mental states. We must not let the cynics of the world analyse our visions to death.

Visions are special, and deserve to be treated with reverence and care.'

'How do you know this?' they asked.

'How do I know? Because I have been gifted a vision. And, around you there will be others who have also received one of these precious gifts. Each will be different, each appropriate to the receiver. Some will be instantly dramatic; with others, it will be years before the receiver understands what they have received.

Shall I share my vision with you?'

They crowded closer, nudging each other, unsure.

'It was many years ago, when I was young and part of a meditation group. One evening we were encouraged to meditate upon love. At first I felt that love was too nebulous a thing to try to focus on, but I tried, and, in time, I felt a change.

My body seemed lighter, somehow, and then I found myself walking through rooms in a building, airy rooms that opened into one another and ultimately out into a garden. It was spring and the garden was full of new flowers and the pale green of new leaves.

I stood in the garden for some time. Then I walked across the grass, and out through a gateway onto a road.

Two people joined me on the road, one on either side, and we walked and talked together. The two were bright with light, their faces shone and their touch was gentle and warm. Eventually they led me off the road, and onto a smaller path which wound through low hills, up into a beautiful clearing in a small wood. There my two companions stood back, and encouraged me to go on by myself.

'I stepped forward – into the love of God.

It was as simple as that – awe inspiring and yet perfectly natural. And, after all these years, that vision is still as bright as it was when I was as young as some of you.'

And they could see the love shining in her eyes.

The Celebration

The Celebration

Brother George had stopped in the town for the night, on his way back from the Great Celebration of the Trinity. However, as he looked around the kind faces of the people who had offered him hospitality, he realised that he had seen very few of them at the celebrations.

He was puzzled. As one who enjoyed his own company and who gained much from quiet times of peace and reflection, he had, never the less, felt drawn to go to the Great Celebration. This was partly because he had been invited, and it seemed to Brother George that it was more than a little discourteous to simply not turn up to a party that had been specially planned and prepared for those who had been invited.

But he went also because it was a great joy to be among a large number of Christians, and he found his faith – a faith that creaked alarmingly like most people's from time to time – he found his faith enriched by the simple act of being among so many fellow pilgrims.

This thought gave him an idea, and, in the morning, before he left, Brother George offered to tell his hosts a story. And this is the story that he told.

'A group of people were on a journey together.

It was a long journey, but they were a large, companionable and friendly group and they looked forward to seeing new places. Some had known each other for many years and deep friendships had developed. Others, who had been in the group for just as long, were more reserved and distant, while others had only recently joined the group and were still feeling their way a little. As with most groups, some were noisy and extrovert, and some were quiet and perhaps rather shy.

Now, the group did not travel together all the time. Some liked to move fast; others more slowly. But, no matter what they had been doing during the day, the whole group came together in the evening to share their experiences. These evenings were special. They served to remind the travellers that they were still part of one group, and that they were all on the same journey.

As time passed , however, some sought a greater degree of independence. Many had places that they wished to see or things that they wished to do that the rest of the group did not seem interested in doing. There were even arguments. So the individual members spent more and more time apart. They began to find that things – always important things – got in the way of their evening meetings. They formed smaller groups and suggested that it made more sense for these smaller groups to meet every night, and for the larger group – the main group – to meet once a week for celebration and thanksgiving.

More time passed, for this was a very long journey. By now the individuals in the smaller groups felt that there were so many very important things to do that, perhaps, they should meet just once a week or at most twice They also decided that the main group only needed to meet three or four times a year.

Eventually the smaller groups spawned yet smaller groups, and the people forgot altogether that they were part of the main group - the group in which they had all started the journey. And so, when they were invited to come together to show that they *were* still part of the greater, original group of travellers, they really couldn't see the point. Indeed some were not sure that they were actually on a journey at all any more. So they stayed at home and assumed that their invitations had been wrongly addressed, and were intended not for them but for someone else.'

'But,' said Brother George, looking at the villagers, 'the invitations were not wrongly addressed. They were meant for *all* the members of even the *smallest* groups, just as the invitations to the Great Celebrations were offered, in love, to all of us.

And the journey has not ceased. It is the journey of faith on which we are all fellow pilgrims. Sometimes the journeying is easy. Sometime it is very hard. We often need help. Our nurture centre is normally our small, local group – our local church – but we should never forget that we are part of a single, great movement with Christ at our head. It is good to be able to share this appreciation sometimes with those from other small groups – especially when someone has taken the trouble to lay on a special party for us'.

Brother George spread his hands.

'Surely,' he asked, 'you are not as ungracious as the people in Luke's Gospel story who thought up all sorts of excuses at the last moment for not going to a party to which they had all been invited? I find it difficult to believe this. But I also find it difficult to match your kindness to me with your apparent discourtesy over the recent celebrations. Perhaps I am missing something. Perhaps you all feel that you have too much church; that you do too much. I don't know. I would prefer, instead, to share with you a reminder of those early days, when the excitement of the journey was at its strongest.'

He read to them from the Acts of the Apostles. Then he rose and took his leave in silence.

The Meal

The Meal

A group of friends were meeting for an evening meal. They were not a terribly honest or upright group. One was an insurance salesman who sold inappropriate policies to people; another was a second-hand car salesman who doctored the mileage on his cars. One was the owner of an infamous night-club. One man ran a sexshop; another was a rather dodgy financial advisor. There was a man who smuggled van loads of beer and wine back from abroad and sold it out of his car boot, so putting legitimate traders out of business.

They met quite regularly together, and perhaps some of the security of the group was based upon the fact that they knew enough about each other to stop anyone from stepping out of line. They certainly did not trust one another.

Now, though, they were talking quietly together, waiting for the last of their group to join them. His name was Matthew, and he was a tax official who was not above taking a backhander to fiddle someone's tax returns for them.

When he finally came, however, he brought someone else with him. He brought Jesus. His friends were horrified. They shuffled in their seats, and looked at one another in embarrassment.

They were angry with Matthew. But Jesus smiled and thanked them for letting him join in their meal.

The group calmed down a little, then began to talk about the sort of things that not-so-close friends often talk about – everything, in other words, but themselves and their own lives. It was a sort of unwritten rule with them, as with so many groups.

Jesus listened, joined in, laughed and made jokes. They all began to relax. Then, imperceptibly, each member of the group realised that they had not only begun to talk about themselves but that they were starting to defend – to excuse – what they did. They were, in fact, responding to two things that were implicit in Jesus' words of fellowship – a sense of challenge and a sense of reconciliation.

It was as if he enabled each of them to say things that they had always wanted to say. In some indefinable way he allowed them to think aloud things that they had felt were best buried. For too long they had all believed that there was no point changing. They were living off their wits, being clever. It was exciting, and anyway, if they didn't do what they did, they would suffer financially. They were used to being ostracised by certain sorts of people, indeed by most people. They were pretty thick skinned.

But Jesus cut through all that. He was very happy to be with them, to accept them as they were. He didn't want them to give up all their old ways before he would sit down and share a meal with them. In fact, the opposite was true. He went out of his way to be where groups were meeting. He loved being with people – all sorts of people. When he was with them he had an opportunity to offer, through love and compassion, a different perspective. He didn't harangue them and he certainly didn't say that he was better than them. But with a raised eyebrow, a look, a question, he encouraged people to look again at themselves and he offered an alternative way forward.

In everything that he did, he brought God into the centre of life. But he also showed that you didn't have to be terribly serious and straight-laced all the time. You could have fun. You could enjoy yourself. You could get pleasure from being *part* of something rather than fighting *against* something all the time.

And the men around that table? Jesus encouraged them to see that, if they simply continued to try to score points for themselves by cheating 'the system', they would end up being able to see nothing of true value through the clouds of deceit that they had wound around themselves.

And, when Jesus got up to leave, at least one of those hard-nosed, cynical, men-of-the-world got up and quietly followed him.

A Night of Wonder

A Night of Wonder

God stormed through the great halls of heaven. He smashed his fists down upon the table and clenched his teeth. He wanted to scream with frustration, but he knew that the scream of God would destroy everything – everything that he had so carefully planned and made.

Instead he slumped down onto his chair and sighed. He was totally and completely exasperated.

'What else can I do? I have given them all that they could possibly wish for – all that their hearts could possibly desire'.

And Wisdom smiled and shook her head.

'You can do nothing more. The next step must be taken by them. They must wish to come to you. You must be patient and allow them to grow, to make their own mistakes, to understand the implications of their own actions. The more you protect them, the more they will take for granted, and the less they will value what you have offered'.

And the Word was silent. He had been working hard through the mouths of the prophets. He was tired, and could think of nothing new to say.

So God waited and watched.

And the people assumed that he had gone away

at last, and that they could get on with life without having to worry about trying to understand the greater picture – the full potential of the relationship that had been offered to them. They preferred to be small-minded and self-centred. They wanted all that they had been given without having to show any gratitude, without having to say thank you.

So they fought and they cheated one another, and they stepped on one another as they climbed the ladders of wealth and privilege and status.

And they said 'I am successful because I am clever and hard working. I simply don't have time to care about those who are obviously lazy and not so naturally talented. I have worked for my luck. Let them do the same'.

Kings fought against kings for acres of fertile land – and they filled the land with devastated cities, burning crops and dead bodies. And they said, 'I am King. I am strong and powerful and I will prove it. Get out of my way'.

The merchants and shop keepers cheated the people, selling inferior goods at inflated prices, and encouraging everyone to feel that they had to own more and more in order to be able to display their status to their neighbours.

The priests devised rituals of greater and greater complexity to cover the emptiness of their prayers – to cover the fact that they had ceased to pray at all except for public display.

And the poor died and the ill starved. And the

dispossessed and refugees wandered homeless until they rotted in some forgotten corner.

And God waited and watched.

And as he watched he saw, among the surging, argumentative crowds, men and women who turned to help their neighbours. He saw honest men and caring women. He saw leaders who ruled with wisdom and brought peace to their lands. He saw merchants who traded fairly, and shop keepers who kept the families of single parents and widows fed through simple acts of kindness.

And deep in his heart he felt the prayers of the priests and the people who remained faithful.

And the love that was in God burned brightly.

God decided that it was time to act.

The Spirit of Wisdom flowed through him, and the Word grew to encompass all that was God, before bursting upon the earth trailing clouds of glory and angels across the sky.

And the Word became flesh and dwelt among us.

Us! Squabbling, petty, violent, greedy, aggressive, selfish, caring, hopeful, intelligent, compassionate, loving humanity.

Here, on earth, the creator of the universe was born in a tiny baby, a child of grace and wonder. A child that tied forever the God of all space and time with the here and now.

The mysterious, distant God became also the God who is beside us and within us all. A god *of* love, who *is* love itself, came to us *in* love and *as* love to offer forgiveness and a new beginning to all who asked.

It is hard to imagine such a thing – God here on earth – but if you have loved, no matter how imperfectly, then the light of God has shone from your eyes. If you have wept, you have known a little of the pain that God carries. If you have laughed, you have become part of the joy of God.

Each year, at Christmas time, we come once more into a night full of mysteries, when time stands still and the walls – the walls that so often seem to blind us to the amazing wonder of creation – are thin. We should reach out and grasp that moment, and hold it close. It is a priceless living jewel.

Feel the excitement of discovering all over again this new life. But do not keep it to yourself. Freely share what has been freely given to you, and watch the wonder grow.

That is what Christmas is. The birth of wonder, reborn each year.

The Gateways

The Gateways

Brother George was not much given to visions. He was, in fact, rather jealous of those who received these wonderful insights. Indeed, when he was feeling particularly uncharitable, he caught himself thinking that some of the experiences were simply made up to impress people. He knew that he was being unfair and mean-minded – indeed he was being unchristian – but no matter how he prayed, he couldn't stop these thoughts from creeping into the dark corners of his mind.

Well, now he had a problem, because there was no way to describe what he had just seen but to say that he had been offered a vision. And he had discovered something else at the same time, that visions have a way of insisting that they are shared.

So, during the time of sharing that those of his fellowship offered one another, he found himself on his feet.

'I saw a great wall with arches built one above the other and many gateways, like an amphitheatre or a football stadium. People were lining up to go through the gates, but the queues were very different in length. One was very short, no more than a handful of people, so I went across to ask what was happening. They told me that it was not a football match but the way into heaven. They admitted that they had been directed towards the short queue, but none of them knew why. To me, however, it was obvious. These quiet, peaceful people were the saints, the truly virtuous. They invited me to join them, but I couldn't even pretend to be as selfless as them. So I walked over to the next queue.

This queue was longer. Many of the people were richly dressed and they were busily engaged in polishing small, discrete silver halos. These people knew exactly why they were there, and they told me without hesitation or what they called false modesty. They were the self-righteous coming to claim their rightful place in heaven. The strange thing was that they didn't seem to notice that they were all passing in through one gate and back out through another in an endless circle. They did not invite me to join them. In fact, they closed up together so that no space was left.

I moved to the next queues. They were much more unruly. People were coming and going, jumping from queue to queue and milling about in some confusion. I watched as a man tapped the woman in front on the shoulder and, when she turned round, he slipped in front of her in the queue. A few minutes later the same man turned round, apologised and went back towards the end of the queue. Before he got there, however, he elbowed his way back in front of a man who was, momentarily, turning to talk to someone in the next queue.

I felt more comfortable among this crowd, and pushed my way into one of the lines. In front of me was an old man carrying a large bag over his shoulder. I was just about to offer to carry it for him, when I realised that I too was carrying a large and heavy bag. It was strange. I hadn't noticed the bag at all until that moment, but, as I gradually got nearer to the head of the queue, the bag got heavier and heavier.

Near the gateways was a booth – a sort of toll booth or ticket office – and in it was sitting Jesus. I recognised him immediately, of course, although he didn't look like any of the pictures. Jesus was not, however, selling tickets. He was simply offering to take each person's bag. Very few words were spoken, but I was amazed at the variety of reactions to Jesus' offer. I saw, too, why there was so much confusion in these queues. Some people gratefully handed over their bags and passed on. Others handed Jesus their bags, and then snatched them back again and ran away from the crowd. Many left the queues as they got closer to Jesus and quietly slipped towards the back again. Some were quiet; some noisy. Many were in tears; many were confused. Some looked puzzled; some pugnacious. But through it all Jesus simply kept making the same offer – 'Let me take your bag from you' – and, to those who handed over their bags, he seemed to say something else.

What was in those bags that would stop so many from giving their bags even to Jesus? I decided to slip out of my queue and sit upon the grass for a bit so that I could look into my bag. I opened it, and tipped the contents out onto the ground. It was full of carefully wrapped parcels, bits of old rope, sharp-cornered boxes, flat packets and envelopes – all sorts of bits and pieces.

One parcel was labelled 'Unreasonable and Uncontrolled Anger'. Another was labelled 'Pride'. There was a very large parcel marked 'Jealousy'. There was a matching blindfold and earplug set marked 'To be used every time you begin to hear or see too clearly'. There was a buff envelope marked 'Broken Promises', and a long tube with 'Self-centredness' written in large letters down one side. One of the ropes had a label attached on which there was a diagram which showed how to tie one's feet together to avoid swift progress in any direction. The rope was made of twisted strands of self-doubt. There was a wooden box full of grudges, shining brightly from frequent polishing.

And there were other things in the bag as well. Things that hurt as I picked them up, but which I couldn't put down. Among them was the Pain of Deeply Buried Sorrows and Bad Memories. There was Frustration, and a whole sheaf of Misunderstandings. There was a bottle of Well-Matured Despair.

I was amazed by some of the things that I was still carrying. I thought that I had lost them or given them away long ago, and yet I packed them all back into my bag with infinite care. Many I recognised as those things that are called sins, although this was by no means true of all the items. I understood, however, what was happening to me and to those around me.

Not far away a woman was also repacking her bag, and we rejoined the queue together as near the back as possible. We both needed time.

Gradually we neared the front of the queue again, the woman just ahead of me. We reached Jesus still sitting quietly in his booth. Tentatively the woman handed over her bag and walked on. Strengthened by her example, I handed over my bag as well.

Jesus smiled. 'Peace be with you, my friend,' he said. Then he put his hands upon my shoulders and said, 'Be still, and know that I am God.'

And there was calm and peace in that gift of stillness.

Then, to my surprise, Jesus lifted me up and gently turned me round.

In a voice full of love and pain, he said, 'If you are willing, there is still work that you can do for me. Will you go through the Gate of Continued Life on Earth, and take with you the blessings of my love to share? Take this love to those of my children who still struggle in the dark, who still believe that they are alone. And when you love,

love with my love. And when you cry, cry with my tears'.

What could I do? I walked through the gateway – and found myself here.'

Brother George sat down. There was a companionable silence.

The Stone and the True Treasure

The Stone and the True Treasure
(A traditional story)

Brother George had reached the outskirts of the village. It was a fine, warm evening, and he was settling down under a tree for the night when a villager came running up to him and said,

'The stone! The stone! Give me the precious stone!'

'What stone?' asked Brother George.

'Last night I had a dream,' said the villager. 'A voice told me that if I went to the outskirts of the village at dusk I should find a Brother who would give me a precious stone that would make me rich forever,'

Brother George laughed. 'Are you sure it was a stone, and not a Lottery ticket?' he asked.

But the man did not laugh. He was so tense with expectation that Brother George felt sorry for him. He rummaged in his bag and pulled out a stone. 'The voice probably meant this one,' he said, as he handed the stone over to the villager. 'I found it on the forest path some days ago. You can certainly have it.'

The man gazed at the stone in wonder. It was a diamond, probably the largest diamond in the whole world. He took the diamond and walked away. All night he tossed about in bed, unable to sleep. Next day at the crack of dawn he woke Brother George and asked, 'Do you know the worth of this diamond?'

Brother George yawned. 'Oh, I have a fair idea. But I have all I need. And you seemed to need the riches of the stone so desperately.'

The villager was quiet for a moment. Then he laid the diamond on the ground in front of Brother George and said, 'Please, share with me the wealth that you have in your heart, the wealth that makes it possible for you to give this diamond away so easily.'

The Sacrifice

The Sacrifice

The man stood in the empty Church. It was cool and dark. He was, I suppose, what we would call a successful man. He had achieved much. He was comfortably well-off. He was happily married and had several children. But he was also troubled. He couldn't sleep. Every night he dreamed a strange dream which was so disturbing that he woke up. He dreamed that he heard a voice calling to him. He knew that it was the voice of God and he followed the sound. He walked across fields and along dusty roads to a great city. The city was full of people, but strangely sad and silent.

He walked through the city streets to the doors of the Church. But there he stopped, because he knew that, once inside, God was going to ask him to make a sacrifice. He knew that the sacrifice was for all those he had passed by. He felt drawn to help them, but he was terribly afraid. Why was he afraid? Because he thought that the sacrifice asked for might be the life of his only son. He loved his son dearly, and he knew that such a sacrifice would be impossible for him to offer. So he turned back from the door of the Church and walked away.

He sought to placate God by offering more

money; by saying more prayers; by giving to the poor.

But each night he dreamed the same dream. Eventually, exhausted by worry and lack of sleep, he came at night to the Church and stepped inside. He knelt in front of the altar and cried, and prayed.

'Lord, I have come, but I cannot offer that which you ask'.

Now, perhaps above everything, the Lord is patient, and he answered:

'But I haven't asked you yet. How do you know what I wish of you?'

'I dreamed, Lord, that you asked me to sacrifice my son for the sake of the people.'

'Ah, no, my friend. No. I have done that myself. I know the pain.'

The man was almost overwhelmed by relief, but this was short lived.

'What I seek from you is your own life.'

The man gulped and was silent.

'But I don't want to *take* your life. I want *you* to live your life to the full, in a way that will help my people to reach their full potential as loving stewards of Creation. That is why I made you. That is why I gave you skills, a lively mind and the ability to love. That is why I was willing to watch my Son sacrifice himself to redeem the sins of mankind, to offer each of you a way back into my arms. But I will never make demands of you. I will only ask if you are willing to try to love my people as my Son loved them? Is this too much to ask? Was my Son worth so little?'

The man was silent for a while, because he was ashamed. Then he asked quietly: 'Will you help me, Lord?'

'Gladly, as I always have.' And the Lord God raised up the man from his knees and breathed on him the fire of the Spirit. Then he sent him back out to renew the world.

Conflict

Conflict

Brother George looked with pleasure at the pages of the fabulous illuminated Gospel. He turned the pages with care, fully appreciative of the rarity of the book that lay open in front of him on the table.

The illuminated pages were famous and stunningly beautiful. One page, the carpet page from the Gospel of Matthew, consisted of a large rectangle with stepped, clasping corners which contained panels of golden interlace. Weaving in and out, back and forward, crossing and re-crossing in highly stylised patterns, this interlace represented the thread of life.

Within the central rectangle, the whole background was covered with a tight, densely packed mass of swaying, curling birds and animals. The creatures had long necks and long bodies, and each was busily biting its neighbour. The colours were predominantly light blue and pink, with small touches of red and green. This image was the very embodiment of conflict.

Brother George remembered being caught up in just such a sea of conflict not many days before as he had fought and weaved his way through the crowds at a large and busy underground station in London. No one was particularly violent or aggressive, but there had been hundreds, probably thousands, of people in a confined space. No one was being overtly unkind or uncaring. They were simply people going home from work. The trouble was that everyone was struggling to go the way they wanted to go, and they were not terribly aware of anyone else.

He sighed and looked again at the illuminated page before him.

Across the central rectangle, with its sea of writhing, biting creatures, lay a great cross painted in red and green. The cross was, itself, full of serpentine bodied creatures. But the whole feeling was calmer. There was still a wonderful complexity to the lives of the creatures, but the closer Brother George looked the more he sensed a different level of symmetry. Movements were slower, less agitated. And many of the exotic creatures actually lay with their heads beside one another. None was biting its neighbour, and despite the wide use of red – the colour of blood and anger – there was an overwhelming sense of peace.

Brother George leaned back in his chair. In this astonishing tour-de-force of early illustration, he saw just how the Cross could change people's lives. How he wished he had had this image in his head when he was in the underground station. This was not the dark cross, the shadow of the cross of pain. This was not a stark reminder of mans' brutality to man – of conflict at its most violently personal. Rather it was the life-changing Cross of Glory, the cross that renews every life that it truly touches. If he had been able to bring this image to mind, he might have been able to share it with some of those around him. He would certainly have been less inclined to give as good as he got. Brother George closed his eyes. For a moment he saw the Cross of Glory laid across the milling crowd, creating an oasis of calm in the whirlwind. Impossible? Who says so?

The Master of Doubt

The Master of Doubt

When I was a young man I had many ideas. I thought that they were so completely original that they should all be written down, so that I would get the credit before they became contaminated by the thoughts of others. I shunned company, and, for ten years, I shut myself away and wrote.

I wrote twelve great volumes and, in my isolation, I believed that they would be considered to be without parallel in the works of erudition. And they were. I was hailed as the most original thinker since original thought. I was fêted by the rich and famous. Students followed me in droves. Academics wrote learned papers about my work. Such was my conceit that I did not even notice that the wisest minds remained silent.

I led a series of public debates and found that I was superior in intellectual skills to the most renowned of my contemporaries. Even the venerable sage Senan merely sat silent during my orations.

Then, gradually, I found that, although I still won all the debates and arguments, I began to disagree with my own conclusions. I tried to hide my consternation, but it was at this point that Senan came quietly to me when I sat alone one evening'.

'You have at last arrived at doubt,' he said, smiling. 'Now you will be able to use your gift to pursue the truth.'

And he was right. Doubt has been a good friend to me as I have tried to truly understand the mysteries that surround us.

While I was content merely to argue with others, I was not really interested in the truth, no matter what I said. The great debating halls are full of people who have no interest in basic simple truths. There is not enough room in the truth for us to outmanoeuvre each other, for us to score points and for us to make others look inferior. I was very good at all these things, but my oratory was less meaningful than the blowing of the wind in the trees.

I understand far less now than I did when I was in my pomp. But the little I understand is of infinitely greater value to me. I have stood on the edge of the abyss of pride. It is an experience that has nothing to recommend it.

Now, my friends, it is late. We should allow enough time at the day's ending to prepare ourselves for the new day, which comes bringing a whole new set of possibilities.

So let us offer ourselves the courtesy of a time of rest, when we can acknowledge that nothing more can be done today. Then, in the morning, with God's help, we may glimpse a little more of the beauty of truth.

The Introductory Film

The Introductory Film

One night Brother George had a dream. He dreamed that he had died and gone to heaven. At the gates of heaven, Peter met him and welcomed him in.

' Nowadays the first thing that we do for newcomers,' said Peter, 'is to show them a short film'.

Brother George was quite pleased. Even heaven was getting up to date. He assumed that the film would be a sort off introduction to heaven, telling him what to expect and what there was to do. So he settled back. He was a bit surprised that there was no one else in the little cinema, but he waited for the film to begin.

The lights dimmed. The film credits appeared.

God's Truly Universal Films
Present

And then the title came up:

The Life and Times of Brother George

The film started with a close-up of a baby that Brother George felt he ought to recognise. He did recognise the little boy, the bigger boy, the teenager, the young man, the older man, and he was pretty sure that he recognised the old man. It was all him. His life passed before his eyes.

Now, time is rather different in heaven – so I understand. So Brother George had no idea how long the film went on for, but, when he came out, he looked rather shocked and sad.

'What's the matter?' asked Peter.

'Well – that film. It was full of good things, but it was also full of nasty, spiteful incidents.'

'Do you mean that they didn't happen?'

'No. I'm afraid they did happen, although I had forgotten them all. But I thought that God forgave us when we did wrong, and that he blotted it out of our record.'

'Ah, my friend,' Peter replied, 'God did forgive you and forget the things for which you asked forgiveness, and, as a result of which, you were willing to change. God forgave you every time you genuinely said sorry to someone that you had wronged. Those things did not appear on the video. They have gone forever. They no longer exist.

'But all those incidents that are still in the video are the acts of meanness or spitefulness; the lies; the cheating; the unresolved anger; the selfishness and self-centredness; the lack of charity; the times when you turned away or walked past someone who needed help; the times when you thought yourself better or more holy than others. All those incidents that are still there, you simply forgot about. You never said sorry. You never did anything to try to put things right. Everyone gets things wrong sometimes, I myself know that only too well. But if you don't ask for forgiveness, how can you receive forgiveness? How can God forgive you?'

Brother George sat down heavily upon a bench – and then he woke up. It had all been dream. He was so relieved. Then he got up, dressed and hurried off to try to put right some of the many things that he had done wrong. He had rather a lot to do, so there was no time to lose.

Then and Now

Then and Now

'But tell us what really happened,' they said.

'Well, after we had taken him down, with the whole world dark about us, we carried him to the tomb and laid him gently in the inner chamber. The soldiers were not unkind. They let us kneel together for a little time, but then they hurried us out, rolled the great stone across the mouth, sealed the stone and stood guard.

And for a while it was as if even God was divided by grief. The living, vibrant presence of God was everywhere except inside the tomb.

But this could not be, and gradually God changed the cold of the tomb to the warmth of a womb, from which new life could come. It was as if God offered warmth like a brooding chicken to a solitary egg. After three days, just as an egg is broken open by the new life inside, so the shell of the tomb was broken open – the stone was rolled away – and our resurrected Lord stepped out and showed himself to us again. We were absolutely stunned. But then, as we were touched by this new light of life, we believed.

And in belief we saw that we were being offered a new start, a new birth, ourselves. And we finally understood what Jesus had been saying for all those years. God was whole again and our Lord was part of the wholeness of God, and so, in a different way, were we. From then on we simply could not stop ourselves. We went out into the world to share our wonderful gift with as many people as possible. That is what brought me to you.'

The people listened and saw the light of joy shining from his eyes, and they too believed.

And so the story was passed on from generation to generation, but strangely, while in each generation some were touched afresh by the amazing glory of the new light that shone upon the world through the open doorway of the empty tomb, others only remembered the image of the egg and they focused on this.

Eventually, for most people, the Easter Egg became the main sign of Easter, stacked high in the shops and promoted in adverts, offering short term pleasure rather than a way to lasting glory.

What strange and rather perverse creatures we humans are, apparently more willing to go for instant pleasure rather than to work at a greater goal.

Or could it be that, in our 'modern' world, we are encouraged to rush by one another so quickly that it is simply no longer possible to see the light shining in someone else's eyes.

What on Earth is Faith?

What on Earth is Faith?

It was the day before he had to make an important decision. Brother George was far from home, and, despite the friendliness of those around him, he felt very alone. After morning prayer with the brothers, Brother George sat on his bed and asked God for a final confirmation that he was doing the right thing. He remained in the quiet of his room for some time.

Then he decided to go out for a walk.

Brother George walked along the road towards the next village, and on the way he came across a vineyard. He went in and simply asked if he could walk through the vines. He wandered through rows of vines heavy with grapes, and remembered Christ's words – 'I am the True Vine'. One row of grapes was blood red.

He walked up over the hill behind the vineyard and lost the path in the short grass on the hill top, but he pressed on and eventually came down to a clearly marked footpath through a collar of trees on the steep side of a valley.

'I am the Way', Christ said.

In the bottom of the valley ran a fast, wide river.

'I am the Water of Life'.

Walking beside the river he met two of the older brothers from the Friary, men full of commitment and the joy of life, who told him that he was going in the right direction.

The walk took several hours and he arrived back at the Friary in time for tea and bread.

'I am the bread of Life', Christ said.

To get back to the Friary Brother George crossed the river on a fairly new bridge and he noticed that the balustrade walls were already cracking. Then, instead of walking up the track on the far side of the bridge, he wandered along the riverbank until, among a tangle of brambles, he found a ruined medieval bridge. The whole bridge had fallen into the river and he watched great sandstone blocks being moved about by the sheer power of the water.

As he looked at the blocks, Brother George saw the fallen bridge as the past, the new bridge as the present and the way across the new bridge as the future. The new bridge also seemed to represent in his mind the church of today – in need of some repair and with only us to repair it so that the road forward can be kept open. And he saw that we – the people of today's church – we are not only the repairers of the bridge; we are the bridge.

So for Brother George a quiet walk through rolling hills became a series of simple but striking affirmations of the step he was about to take in faith. They were treasures and he carried them carefully with him the following day. He had never before experienced such a showering of so many faith enhancing experiences all at once. He realised that he might never again, but when he more fully understood what had been gifted to him, he felt both humbled and exited.

Faith is unquantifiable. It is not that some people have lots and others none. Faith is God's gift to all, but far too many of us will not allow the gift to be fully activated. It is as if we were given a television set but refused to allow it to be turned on in case we enjoyed the pictures on the screen, or as if we only allowed ourselves to look at the pictures but kept the sound turned off. Or perhaps it is as if we received, as a present on our birthday, an electric fire, but we only ever ran it on the lowest possible thermostat setting – for fear of getting warm.

The Life of Faith is a journey and the road Faith takes us down does not always pass through dramatic scenery. Sometimes our surroundings will be fairly dull, sometimes bleak, but just as often we can be lifted up by the joy of the unexpected.

The church of Christ is a Pilgrim Church and no member of Christ's church can stand still for ever. If we ask for guidance God will offer us clear signs in response to our prayers. It is, however, abundantly clear throughout the Bible, and from the experience of every Christian who has ever written about their faith, that such responses are not always instantaneous. When they are they carry a special wonder for us. When they are not, we need to remember that we have, in fact, been given so much more than any of the leaders or prophets of the Old Testament. Each of us has been given the greatest of all signs of God's love and commitment – through the life, the ministry and the resurrection of Jesus Christ.

Open Your Eyes

Open Your Eyes

Jesus sat down on a rock and said:

'For heaven's sake, stop worrying all the time. You worry about what you can and can't eat; whether you should diet; what is good to drink. And if you're not worrying about your food, you worry about what you should wear.

Life is brim-full of things that are much more important and interesting than boring discussions about food and cloths'.

Look outside. Do you see the birds, the sparrows and starlings, the robin and the blackbird. They don't grow things. They don't have silos full of grain, or cupboards crammed with tins, or freezers packed to the brim. And yet God doesn't let them all starve. He offers them the riches of creation. Don't you think that he will do at least as much for you?

The same goes for your clothing. Think about the flowers in your garden or in the park. Think about the apple blossom and the spring crocuses, the bluebell woods and red roses. They don't work all day to buy more and more fancy clothes, and yet they are more beautiful than the most glamorous model wearing the most stunning designer creation.

Be happy with who you are. Enjoy what God has given you. Enjoy being yourself. You are unique and special.

And tell me this. What on earth is the point of worrying about what might happen tomorrow. Oh, I understand the need to plan ahead, but don't let this overwhelm your life. *Now* is a very important time. Do you think that you can make your life longer by worrying. Far from it, my friends. If you're stressed out all the time, worrying about the future, you will probably make your life shorter. So try to relax a little.

You know what the real problem with people today is? Far too many of you are caught up with chasing things that the world considers important – with keeping up with the latest fashions; with demanding the latest toys; with buying bigger houses or a car with the latest number plate; with going on ever more expensive holidays, so that you can boast to your friends. You measure success by what you can pile up around you. But this is all pointless. These things are like dust in the wind, they blind you for a moment and then they blow away.

And while you are blinded you can't see your neighbours, your friends, those you love. So you don't see the neighbour who need help. You don't see the hand held out in friendship. You can't look into the eyes of love, and see love being offered in return'.

Open your eyes, my friends, and live.'

Hidden Beauty

Hidden Beauty

Long ago, in a land far away, a group of rather pious aesthetes came together to set up a small community in the desert. Some of the members of the community were skilled stone carvers and they began to carve a series of religious diptychs (that is two panels that can be folded out to display two related images side-by-side). These diptychs were of high quality, and gradually the artists were encouraged to think of their carvings as more than simply beautiful.

They declared that the images were filled with a special power, but that the carvings only retained this power while they were secret. The artists felt that each time the panels were opened the images lost some of their power, especially when they were seen by people from outside the closely knit community group.

So they began to carve diptychs which were then permanently sealed. Thus only those few who had seen the images could possibly say what they were. This development was reflected in the name by which the community became known – the Apocryphal Community of the Petrified Introverts.

Eventually, one of the Master Carvers, known only as the Master of Internalised Realisation, developed the community's ideas in a truly amazing way.

The master taught his followers to carve on the inside of blocks of stone through a hole no bigger than a small pencil. They carved scenes of staggering complexity and beauty actually inside small, unbroken slabs of stone. No one, not even the carver, saw the completed image and, therefore, the power of the carving could be preserved completely intact.

Sadly the community did not long survive the completion of the first few of these artistic marvels. All too soon, jealousy, masquerading as philosophy, split the group into opposing factions.

The Mystics said that even the act of carving sullied the ultimate purity of the beauty that lay in the mind, and that stone was simply too base a material to contain true power.

The Cynics believed that the carvers were no more than charlatans, seeking ways to enhance their second rate skills.

The Critics wondered whether beauty that could not be seen could ever be truly classified, and suggested that, surely, there had to be an interaction between the object and the observer before anything could be said to be beautiful. They did not mention power at all.

The Realists stated that power and beauty were opposites, and that they cancelled each other out when brought together. Therefore, there could not be anything of true worth inside the stones.

The Master Carver listened in silence to the babble of opposing voices. Then he picked up the completed carvings and walked out into the desert. When he was quite alone, he knelt down and carefully broke each stone into two. Then he closed his eyes and opened the two halves of the broken stones, so that the sun shone on the carving.

Briefly he opened his eyes and looked at the play of light and shadow across the delicate details. Then he closed his eyes again.

In that moment he realised that it had been an act of astonishing arrogance to try to keep hidden the beauty that the carvers had created. The true, the only, power that the carvings possessed lay in their ability to inspire and delight others, and, far from being diminished by being open to all, this power grew with each new sharing.

After some time, the Master Carver opened his eyes again and he saw that the whole world was beautiful and full of power.

And he felt more than a little foolish, and also greatly blessed.

The Fork in the Road

The Fork in the Road

'Halt. Who goes there?'

'Who are you?'

'What sort of traveller are you. Its obvious who I am. I am the standard ancient guard at the fork in the road. You have to ask me questions or answer a riddle, before you can go any further. Today I've run right out of riddles, so questions will have to do.'

'What sort of questions?'

'I'm not here to tell you what sort of questions. You are supposed to tell me what you are seeking and then ask which way you should go'.

'Oh, I see. I'm rather new to all this'.

'So I see. Well, what do you seek?'

'I seek answers'.

'To what? Don't you have to know the questions first?'

'I believe that in the past mankind has known many valuable things that have now been forgotten. I want to find these aspects of our past again'.

'Ah. Then you will want that smelly, dirty, plague-ridden path over there. The one that is all dark and overgrown, with the big signs saying 'No entry' and 'One-way traffic only' on it'.

'No, I don't want to go back into the past'.

'Just as well'.

'I seek to go forward by following my own footprints on the pathway that leads back through mankind's collective amnesia'.

'How pretentious you are'.

'But it's difficult to explain in simple terms'.

'Pretentiousness merely gets in the way of clear thinking'.

'But I believe that, as we have become more sophisticated, we have lost all sorts of knowledge and skills, and I would like to rediscover them'.

'And why do you think that you are more sophisticated than your ancestors?'

'Because their lives were simpler. They didn't know as much. They weren't as well educated as we are. Medicine was primitive. They had to fight for their land'.

'Do you know, I didn't realise that we had done away with war. I must have missed that. When did it happen?'

'Now you're being facetious'.

'Oh, sorry I'm sure. Look, you have just gone through a list of reasons for leaving the past where it is. You are confused and you clearly do not understand the difference between sophistication and the tinsel that decorates the spiky bits of modern society. You're in no fit state to travel anywhere. So you can either stay here, or go down the left fork. You will find that that road takes you back to where you were. And when you have learned that our ancestors were every bit as sophisticated as us, then you can try again to find out what they can teach us.

And with that the ancient guard dropped his huge spear across the right fork in the road, and fell asleep.

Images and Symbols

Images and Symbols

Brother George was visiting a friend who was an artist. He knocked on the door and his friend answered.

'Ah, the very man. Come in. Come in.'

They walked together through into a small, airy studio.

The artist made coffee for them both, and they sat down at his paint-spattered table.

'My friend, I have a problem. You might be able to help'.

Brother George tried to look encouraging, while wondering what was going to come next.

'For some time I have been working on a detailed rough for a painting of the Archangel Gabriel visiting Mary to tell her that she has been chosen to bear the Christ child. We live in such a visual age, and I have been trying to create an image that I felt drew on the past, but belonged to our own time.'

'Wonderful. May I see it?'

'Well, that is the problem. It's not finished. Something is not right, but I can't work out what it is'.

The artist got up and brought a coloured drawing to the table.

Within a curving border, Gabriel was drawn as a figure of light with golden yellow features, against the brightness of the sun. He was surrounded by a great diamond-shaped nimbus, a halo, that spread out into the deep blue of the sky. From the nimbus around Gabriel fell a twin column of golden, nail-headed star-shapes, to be caught up into a swirling vortex.

'These represent the Spirit of God descending,' the artist explained.

Brother George nodded. 'And the nail-heads in these stars, they are there to acknowledge the Cross that is to come?'

'Yes. They are the beginning and the end'.

Below the vortex the artist had drawn a highly schematised Mary. Her head was recognisable, staring up in profile, but the rest of her had become a complex, patterned series of interlocking shapes.

'I finished this drawing weeks ago, and I went on to get the board ready for the painting. But I am not happy. I get the drawing out and stare at it, and put it away again. But I cannot see what needs to be changed.'

The artist drew his hand through his hair, and looked at Brother George with an exasperated smile.

'Any ideas, brother?'

Brother George looked again at the picture and after some time, he said:

'One thought does come to me'.

'Um?'

'I wonder if it is the figure of Mary that is troubling you?'

'Why do you say that?'

'Well, although all the other elements in the picture can only be represented by symbols, Mary was a human being. She was not just a symbol and, in a way, you have diminished her humanity by the way that you have drawn her. Mary was a very special lady, but not because she symbolised something'.

'Why then?'

'I think that she was unique because, as a result of being willing to trust, being able to accept and believe Gabriel's astonishing message, and by being prepared to literally take into herself what must have seemed an impossible burden, she bore and gave birth to the Son of God'.

'Through Mary's generosity of spirit, the hands that flung the stars across the sky became the hands of a baby – reaching out to break through our world weariness, our selfishness, our fear, to touch our hearts and our compassion'.

'Careful, Brother George,' the artist grinned. 'You're in danger of turning into a poet'.

'Oh, my friend, this is amazing stuff. It is as if, by being one with a human baby, God sought to reawaken the essential part of each one of us that is also God. God wants to show us that we are not separated from his creation. We are part of it. And the creation is a growing, living part of God'.

'Are you saying that each of us is human and divine?'

'As children of God's creation, I believe that we must be'.

'So I should try to draw Mary as an ordinary young Jewish woman, through whom the divinity of God shone in a very special way'.

'Can you do that?'

'I'm not at all sure that I can,' laughed the artist. 'But you are absolutely right. That is what is needed. Brilliant! This calls for a celebration. Come on, my friend, I will treat you to a meal at my favourite Italian restaurant'.

'That,' said Brother George, with a twinkling smile, 'sounds like a perfectly divine idea'.

The Towpath

The Towpath

The man walked along the towpath beside the canal.

It was nine months since he had lost a very good friend, someone whom he had known nearly all his life. She had died so suddenly that there had been no time to prepare for her death, and, he still felt confused and deeply saddened. He also felt angry, especially with God.

'Why?' he caught himself saying, over and over. 'Why? Why her? She was so kind and generous, and she had so much still to offer.'

Everything seemed to be black, deeply unfair and impossible to understand.

Today, however, something had encouraged him to come to this quiet canal. He didn't know what had first put the idea into his mind, but he remembered that it was a peaceful place.

The man sighed and walked on. After about a mile he came to a tunnel through a steep, wooded hill, and the towpath stopped abruptly. He stood for a while, irresolute and unhappy, with his hands balled into fists in his coat pockets.

Eventually, he decided that he needed to walk on, so he left the water's edge and climbed up the slope. But there was no obvious path over the top.

In the distance, on the crest of the hill, he saw a great mound. He wondered if the mound might surround an air vent for the tunnel because, if so, it would indicate which way the tunnel was going under the hill. So he walked towards it and climbed up the heap. There was no air vent, but behind the mound was a stile and a well worn footpath that had been completely hidden from view.

He remembered his dead friend telling him that, sometimes, even things that get in the way of the path we are trying to follow can be used as markers for a journey.

But she had been talking about a journey into faith.

The man smiled to himself as he remembered how his friend used everyday things, like this footpath hidden behind a pile of rocks and earth, to try to help people to take the next step forward into deeper faith. He remembered, too, the time when she said that the thoughts and images that she was able to share were simply gifts - God's gifts.

Suddenly he realised that he was thinking of his friend as she had been, and not through a cloud of pain. Something was beginning to lift the smothering blanket of grief, and, at that moment, he understood that God had not turned his back. God was with him. God understood all about grief.

The man climbed down the mound, and resumed his walk in a noticeably lighter mood.

The footpath kept branching off in all directions, but, at each branch, only one route was not closed by a gate. He followed the ungated path and eventually he came back down to the canal - quiet and tranquil in the middle of the reds and yellows of autumnal woodland.

He stood by the water and, in his head, he heard his friend laugh and say:

'Of course had you been in a boat, you could have floated through the tunnel. There would have been no risk at all then that you might lose your way'.

And he saw that each of us who embarks on a journey in faith is almost certain, at some time, to encounter blackness and tunnels when we cannot see the way forward. If we only walk *beside* God's love, at such moments of decision or crisis we can get lost. With the help of God, acting through our friends, we may eventually find our way back onto the pathway. But the cost can be high.

If, however, instead of walking beside the flow, we can launch a boat of faith – no matter how frail or small – onto the water, then God's love will carry us through the blackness until we come out again into the sunshine.

'Thank you', the man said, to God – and to his friend. Then he walked on.

Late Beginnings

Late beginnings

The trees had stayed green throughout October and into November, but at last the ground was covered with freshly fallen leaves. Brother George kicked through the leaves like a child, until he slipped and nearly fell on a patch of leaves that were compacted and wet with rain. Then he decided to behave a little more like a mature and sensible adult – well, like an adult of mature years anyway.

He loved the colours of autumn – reds, browns, and yellows against the greens and blues of the evergreens. He remembered walking along a valley some years before, and being almost overwhelmed by the beauty of the wooded hillsides.

There was bonfire smoke in the air, and mist hanging over the river. But there was also the expectation of darkening evenings, morning frosts, and grey days of rain. Each year autumn heralded a time of closing down, of endings, of basking in memories rather than the sunshine.

And then, just as the year began to go to sleep, the church took everyone by surprise by starting to celebrate new beginnings – the advent of a new year. Advent – those precious weeks of anticipation when Christians are encouraged to start looking beyond the autumn mists towards the coming of the great light at Christmas.

On the cusp of the seasons – the change from autumn's wonderful generosity to the pinch-nosed sharpness of winter – right there is where each year the church began its annual pilgrimage of renewal. The pilgrimage will take it through glory and pain to wonder – and beyond. This was a magical time for Brother George, a time of waiting and preparing.

It was also the time of year when Brother George tried to focus of two aspects of God that sometimes seemed to be in conflict with one another. God's wonderful generosity was like the fruitfulness of Autumn, while the harshness of some statements concerning aspects of God's justice seemed to be more like the numbing chill of winter when, which ever way we turn, we cannot get out of the wind.

Brother George remembered the countless words of love that Jesus had shared with his disciples and with the crowds; the innumerable acts of healing and compassion. And he thought again of the simply unbelievable willingness of Christ – God in man – to accept pain and death for us, so that our eyes and hearts might be opened to the power of redemption and salvation.

Against this he set Jesus' warning of the coming day of judgement, when the Son of Man will come in the clouds of heaven with power and great glory. Then all the people of the earth will have cause to mourn, as the elect are gathered in from the four winds while many are swept aside as they were in the flood. 'Therefore', says Jesus, 'you must be ready, for the Son of man is coming at an unexpected hour'.

These stark words have always been unpalatable to some, but what were they actually saying?

Some lines from one of the great prophecies came the Brother George's mind:

> 'He shall judge between nations
> and shall arbitrate for many people.
> They shall beat their swords into ploughshares
> and their spears into pruning hooks,
> Nation shall not lift up sword against nation
> neither shall they learn war any more'.

For a moment, Brother George allowed himself to imagine a world in which this had already happened. He saw just how differently people would feel if, instead of doubt and fear and blood on the stones, there was peace. In such a world there would be no room for those who wished to continue to wallow in their greed, their selfishness, their corruption. He saw the results of people's willingness to change – to wake from sleep, to lay aside the works of darkness and to put on the light.

So, to Brother George, Jesus seemed not to be threatening so much as to be simply stating the consequences of continuing wilful blindness. Few can be unaware of the love that God has showered on the world, and the glory that a living covenant would bring to the world. No one can be unaware of the results of selfishness, of brutality, and of people's unwillingness to follow the simplest of rules – love God and love your neighbour as yourself.

If an agreement is kept by one party and continually flouted by the other, then it ceases to be a viable agreement, and the potential that lies at the heart of the contract will never be realised. And eventually the Lord, who offers us a very particular contract – a covenant so that his love would be able to grow – the Lord may decide that enough is enough. We, who have been given a crucial place in the wonder of creation, may simply run out of time.

So, if humanity is going to change, we need to begin *now*. Tomorrow may be too late.

This, for Brother George, is what Jesus is saying. Tomorrow may be too late. The Kingdom has already come near. *Now* is the time to change.

Brother George picked up a fallen leaf and laid it on the palm of his hand. This year, perhaps even more than in any previous year, he wanted people to stop and think. He wanted Advent to be a time for reflection and proper preparation. He looked at the beautiful fallen leaf and, for a few moments, he allowed it to become a focus for his thoughts. Just two or three minutes, the length of time many people are prepared to offer in memory of the dead on Remembrance Day. And after this short time of quiet, he went back to his work.

But, whenever he had an opportunity, he suggested to other people that they, too, should allow themselves just a few minutes each day to be quiet and reflective. Maybe people could even use some of those minutes to begin to learn how to pray. No one is so pressured, so busy, so crucial, so irreplaceable, that they cannot spare a few minutes each day.

And from these times of quiet new seeds might grow, new understanding, and new hope. And hope is very infectious. Then, who knows, when the Son of Man comes the world might be ready to rejoice and be glad.

The Last Prayer

The Last Prayer

Once upon a time in a village far away from here, there lived a quiet, unassuming woman. She lived with her old mother in a small house with a long narrow garden that ran down to a stream.

The quiet woman enjoyed her garden, and the stream. She was friendly to her neighbours, and most people liked her. Very few, however, would have said that they knew her well.

But the quiet woman became very, very important, and I will tell you why.

Each day the quiet woman would join her mother, and they would pray together. They prayed for the world, for people who were ill, for their friends, and for their neighbours. They prayed for people in trouble, and they often prayed for people who caused trouble. They prayed for the young and the old, for the charitable and for the greedy. They prayed for those who travelled and those who were housebound. They offered prayers of thanksgiving for the wonders that they saw around them, and for each day's blessings. They remembered to give thanks on the days when there seemed little to be thankful for, as well as on the days of plenty.

And the quiet woman and her old mother

assumed that other people prayed as well. After all, most were equally blessed. It was a reasonable assumption, but they were wrong as we shall see.

Now, there came a day when the quiet woman's mother died peacefully in her sleep. The evening before, the old woman realised that death was near. So she asked her daughter to pray with her, and she encouraged her to continue to pray.

The quiet woman was very upset by her mother's death, and she was caught up in the harsh pain of grief for many months. During this time she felt empty, lost and deserted. A blackness swirled through her mind which made her angry, and she cried out against God. She found prayer to be almost impossible and she seldom got beyond 'Why?'

In time, however, the pain gradually began to lessen, and the quiet woman found that she could ask for help in her prayers. She discovered afresh the pleasure that she got from listening to the stream at the end of her garden, from watching the light reflected on the swirling, bubbling water. She began to enjoy being in her garden, and talking to neighbours. She went to the shops and, in her quiet, unobtrusive way, she learned of people's joys and problems.

And each day she set aside time for prayer. It was not always the same time each day; that didn't matter. She began by giving thanks for the day, and for the glorious diversity of creation.

Even on dull or rainy days there was always something, some good news, for which to be thankful.

Then she asked God to hold in his arms those who were in pain or distress, those who were confused, or angry, or grieving. She prayed for the people that she knew, and for those who were hurting but whom she did not know. She prayed for those who were affected by war, and for those who led their people into conflict. She prayed for those who did not have enough to eat, and for those who stole food from the starving to sell for personal gain. She prayed for vulnerable children and pensioners, and for men and women who had to work too hard or who had no work. She prayed for those who had fallen in love and for those who had lost love.

She prayed for those who were naturally generous and for those who were mean and grasping, for the open-handed and the tight-fisted, for the selfless and the selfish. She prayed for those who were able to give and share, and for those who were only able to take. She prayed for those who were thought to be beautiful and for those who were thought to be ugly. She prayed for the many people who were unhappy with their physical appearance and for those who did not know how to be truly themselves.

These times of prayer were important to the quiet woman, but they were not always rich and rewarding. There were days when she felt that she was talking to herself, days when a particular sadness overwhelmed the good things and made the world seem bleak and uncaring. There were days when she could not concentrate and her mind wandered onto everyday worries and insistent trivia. But there were also days when she felt a ripple of warmth pass through her as she stilled herself, times when she simply allowed herself to be carried.

Time passed. The quiet woman grew old. Her neighbours were kind to her as she became increasingly frail, and they looked after her.

But they did not pray for her, because the quiet woman was the last person in the world to pray.

All her neighbours, and everyone else in the world, left someone else to do the praying. They said that they couldn't see the point or that they didn't know how to pray, and they never bothered to learn or to ask.

So, when the quiet woman died, there was silence.

And God, who loved to hear the music that flowed from every corner of his creation, realised that the special music, which came from the voices of the Children of Earth, had been stilled. He was saddened, and the joy within creation was dimmed by his sadness. And the glory of creation, with which God had been so pleased, was lessened.

As a result, the People of Earth found it hard to sing. They found it hard to love. They stopped being inspired, and, although they still ate and drank and moved through their lives from birth to old age, everything became rather dull and monotonous. They knew that something important and special had gone from their lives, but they didn't know what it was and they didn't know what to do to bring it back.

But the quiet woman's last prayer was that others would also learn to value prayer. God heard that prayer, as he hears all prayers, and he hoped that one of her neighbours had also heard the prayer. He gently encouraged them to remember the dying woman's words and to wonder what they might have meant. And he waited.